For Ben, Ted and Will - A&C Guillain

EGMONT
We bring stories to life

First published in Great Britain 2016 by Egmont UK Limited
The Yellow Building, 1 Nicholas Road, London W11 4AN

www.egmont.co.uk

Text copyright © Adam and Charlotte Guillain 2016
Illustrations copyright © Lee Wildish 2016

The moral rights of the authors and illustrator have been asserted.

ISBN 978 1 4052 7362 6 (Paperback)

A CIP catalogue record for this title is available from the British Library.

Treats
FOR A
T. REX

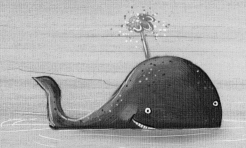

Adam & Charlotte Guillain   Lee Wildish

EGMONT

A boy called George had a staggering thought,
That a **T. rex** could still be **ALIVE**!

So he built a **hang glider** and packed up his bag,
With the tools he would need to survive.

George looked at his map and called, "Trixie - let's go!
We'll need all of your tricks when we're there."

Then his dog did a backflip and jumped in the bag,
And the friends glided off through the air.

They soared over cities and far out to sea,

Till a **strange island** came into view!

An **enormous volcano** rose out of the mist

And down to its summit George flew.

When they came in to land, Trixie
spotted a **ball**
And she leapt out of George's backpack.
But what she unearthed was a very
large egg
That suddenly started to . . .

CRACK!

"It's a **dinosaur egg!**"
shouted George, "and it's HUGE!"
Trixie barked as it rolled all about.
Could it be that a **T. rex** was
going to hatch?

No - a pterosaur baby popped out!

The **pterosaur's mother**

swooped down with a squawk,

George knew he had only one chance.

"Quick, Trixie," he shouted,

"Let's teach them a **trick . . .**"

And the pterosaurs learned how to **dance!**

But as George rewarded them all with a **treat**,

From above came a strange munching sound.

"Trixie - look out!" shouted George in alarm . . .

As a huge foot crashed down on the ground!

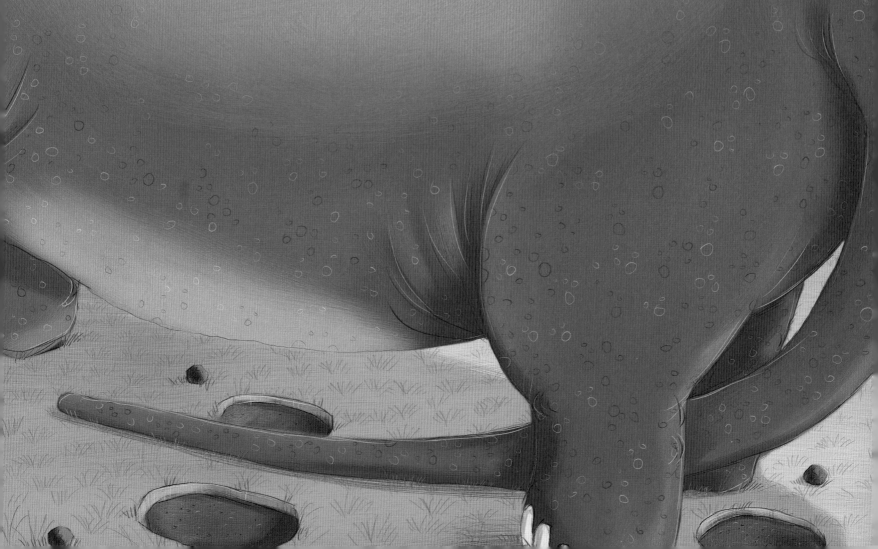

"A massive diplodocus!"
George gasped in awe.

Then he gulped as it lifted its leg.

As quick as a flash, George

called out to his dog . . .

Who taught it to
sit up and beg!

"These dinosaur tricks are **amazing**," cheered George,

And diplodocus grinned as it sat.

But just as the thrill of success made George smile . . .

A tail hit the mud with a SPLAT!

A grumpy triceratops glared down at George,
Then widened its jaws at full stretch!
George picked up some sticks and he looked at his dog –
"Come on, Trixie!" he said . . .

"Let's play fetch!"

Triceratops playfully joined in the game,

But, fed up, George slumped to the ground.

He'd come on this mission to find a T. rex...

Then he heard a **loud stampeding sound!**

And into the clearing there burst a great herd
Of **terrified** small dinosaurs.

"Something scary is coming!"
George called to his dog,
Then he heard the most terrible...

ROAR!

"A T. rex at last!"

shouted George with a whoop,

Then it opened its jaws for a snack.

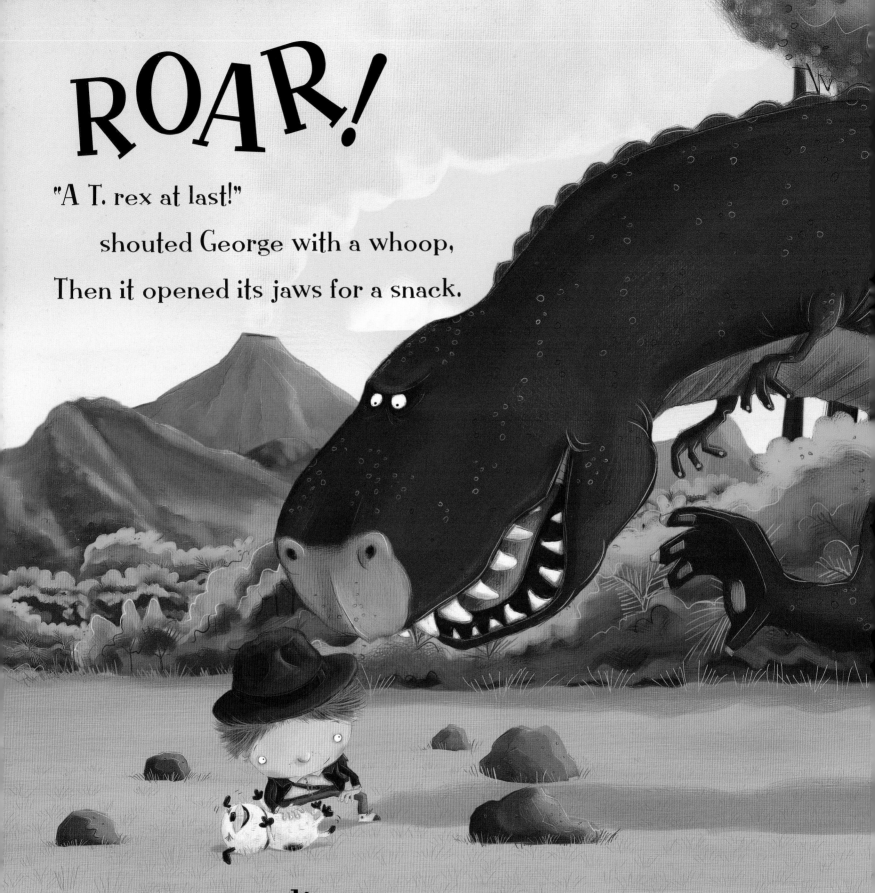

"It thinks we're for **dinner!**" George stammered in fear.

Just then Trixie rolled on to her back.

"Really?" George asked, as he tickled her tum,

How he hoped that her plan wouldn't fail . . .

The **T. rex** just snorted and tilted its head,
Before . . .

...rolling and wagging its tail!

"Clever Trixie!" cried George, as he threw her a treat,

Then he lifted his hand and said "SIT!"

The T. rex obeyed and George had an idea,

"I know what to do – let's train it!"

So George and his dog taught the **T. rex** to stay,

And they trained it to **jump** over sticks.

And with **yummy treats** all the dinosaurs learned . . .

How to do perfect **prize-winning tricks!**